5/2003

GET TO WORK TRUCKS!

by
Don Carter

ROARING BROOK PRESS

Brookfield, Connecticut

In the morning, trucks go to work.

One, two, three, four.
Big trucks, little trucks.

Five, six, seven, eight.
Orange trucks, red trucks,
green trucks, yellow trucks.

These trucks have work to do.

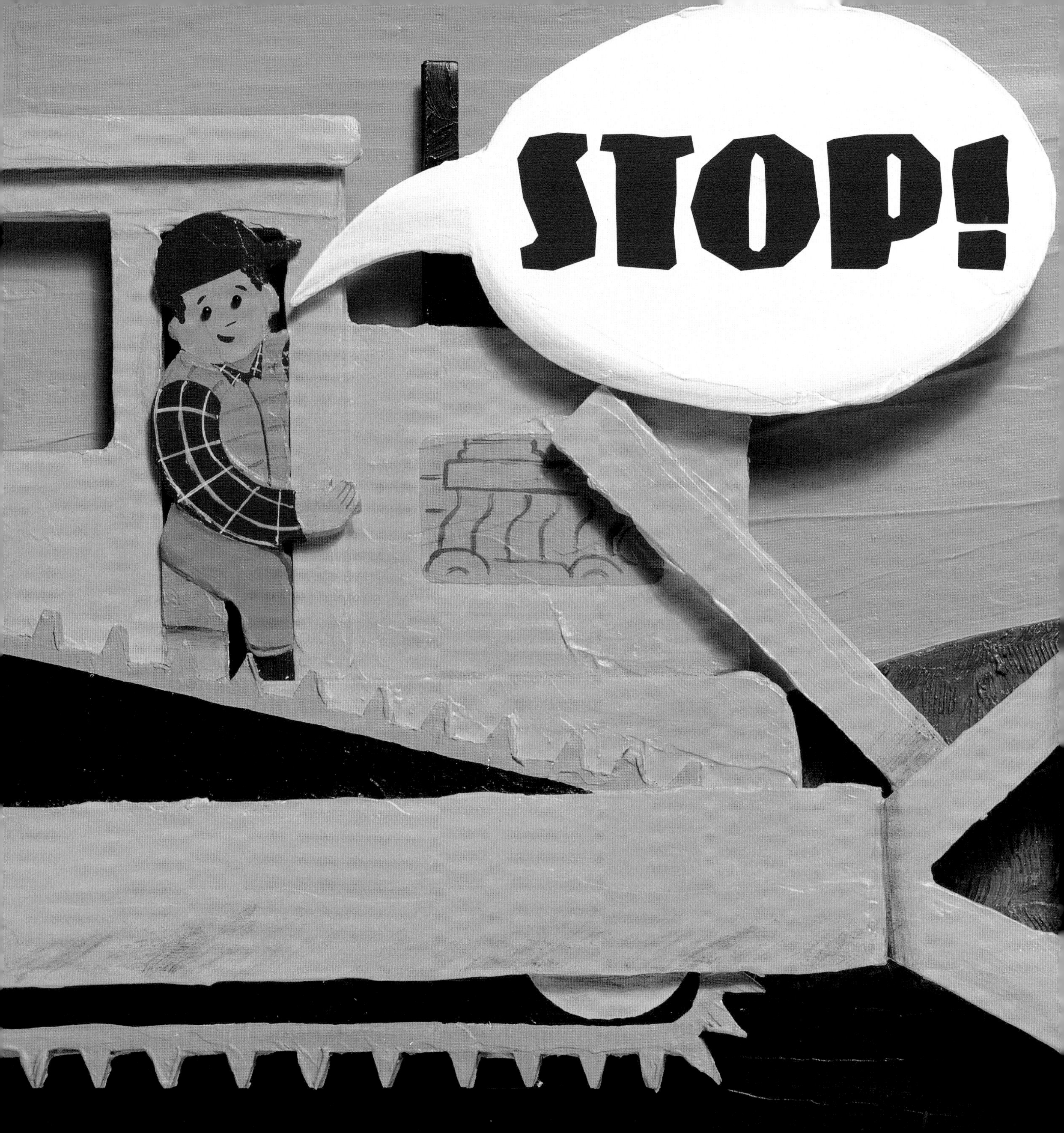
STOP!

Trucks not moving.

Trucks not working.

Get to work, trucks!

The loader lifts a big rock.

The dump truck drops a pile of little rocks.

The digger digs a hole.

And the bulldozer fills a hole.

The cement mixer mixes
and mixes.

Uh, oh! The tow truck fixes.

The crane lifts the beam up high.

The roller flattens the road down low.

Big trucks,
little trucks.

They work
all day long.

Until the work is done.

And in the evening,
trucks go home.

For my little Phoebe. —D.C.

Copyright © 2002 by Don Carter

Published by Roaring Brook Press, a division of The Millbrook Press,
2 Old New Milford Road, Brookfield, Connecticut 06804.

Library of Congress Cataloging-in-Publication Data
Carter, Don. 1958—
Get to work trucks! / Don Carter
     p.   cm.
Summary: Shows a typical day for a group of working trucks: a loader, a dump
truck, a digger, a bulldozer, a cement mixer, a tow truck, a crane, and roller.
[1. Trucks—Fiction. 2. Construction equipment—Fiction.] I. Title.
PZ7.C2432 Ge 2002
[E]—dc21   2001041716

ISBN   0-7613-1543-8 (trade edition)
         0-7613-2518-2 (library binding)

Printed in Hong Kong

10 9 8 7 6 5 4 3 2